PUPPY PATROL™

CHARLIE'S CHOICE

JENNY DALE

Illustrations by Mick Reid
Cover illustration by Michael Rowe

AN
APPLE
PAPERBACK

SCHOLASTIC INC.
New York Toronto London Auckland Sydney
Mexico City New Delhi Hong Kong Buenos Aires

SPECIAL THANKS TO CHERITH BALDRY

No part of this publication may be reproduced, in whole or in part, or stored in a retrieval system, or transmitted in any form or by any means, electronic, mechanical, photocopying, recording, or otherwise, without written permission of the publisher. For information regarding permission, write to Macmillan Publishers Ltd., 25 Eccleston Place, London SW1W 9NF Basingstoke and Oxford.

ISBN 0-439-32022-4

All rights reserved. Published by Scholastic Inc., 557 Broadway, New York, NY 10012, by arrangement with Macmillan Children's Books, a division of Macmillan Publishers Ltd.

12 11 10 9 8   7/0

Printed in the U.S.A.   40
First Scholastic printing, October 2002

CHAPTER ONE

"Isn't he lovely?" said Sarah Parker.

She squatted on the floor of the pen and let Charlie, the golden retriever puppy, scramble over her, giggling as he licked her face and pushed his cold black nose into her neck. He was a lively little dog with a creamy coat and big paws.

"He's going home today," Sarah's older sister, Emily, told her as she carefully set down Charlie's food bowl.

"He can't!"

Their brother, Neil, grinned at them. Five-year-old Sarah never wanted any of the dogs to leave King Street Kennels. "Don't worry, he's coming back soon. His mom, Tansy, is going to a lot of shows over the next few weeks, and Charlie's too little to go with her."

"So we'll be seeing lots more of Charlie," said Emily, picking the puppy up to give him a cuddle.

"Good," said Sarah. "He's my best dog *ever*."

Neil shook his head, laughing. "They're *all* your best dogs ever, Squirt."

Neil, Emily, and Sarah Parker lived in the small country town of Compton, where their parents, Bob and Carole, ran a boarding kennel and rescue center. Charlie was one of the youngest puppy guests they had ever had, and all the Parkers wanted to make sure his stay was a happy one.

The door at the end of Kennel Block Two opened

and Carole Parker's head appeared. "Come on, you three," she said. "You're going to be late for school."

Emily put Charlie down with his nose in front of his food bowl and waited for Sarah to give him a final pat. Then she followed Neil out, closing the door of the pen carefully behind her. Outside in the yard they waved to Kate McGuire, the Parkers' full-time kennel assistant, who was heading for Kennel Block One with more food bowls. She called out something, but her words were drowned by the roar of a loud engine near the side of the house.

Neil paused to watch as a truck backed up past the front of the barn and started to lower a large yellow Dumpster in front of the rescue center. Eddie Thomas, a local builder, was waving his arms and shouting directions.

King Street Kennels was expanding. The Parkers were using money that Bob had recently inherited to build a new rescue center. The old rescue center was going to be renovated into a dog clinic.

A section of fence had been taken out next to the side gate, so that there was room for the builder's trucks to come and go. Their wheels had churned the ground to mud and plowed it into long tracks. Splintered wood and pieces of pipe were scattered all over the site.

"What a mess," Neil murmured to himself.

Past the barn and the old rescue center, the new building was taking shape. Neil had never seen anything quite like it. It was round with a sloped roof and brick columns that alternated with the mesh of the outside dog runs. Inside, when it was finished, there would be pens for fifteen dogs.

"It's like slices of a cake," Bob had explained when he first showed Neil the plans. "It's the latest design."

The Dumpster settled to the ground and the truck moved away. Neil strolled over to stand beside Eddie. "Hello, Mr. Thomas. How's it going?"

Eddie Thomas grinned at him. He was a small, middle-aged man with thinning blond hair. He had first worked for the Parkers when he rebuilt their barn after a fire. Now he was in charge of their current building project.

"Pretty good, Neil," Eddie Thomas replied. "Next week we'll be ready to start on the inside of both buildings."

"Will it be finished in time?" Neil asked. "We've scheduled the opening for two weeks from Saturday."

"Don't you worry," Eddie said. "Your dad and I have figured all that out. Everything's on schedule."

"Cool!" said Neil.

Leaving Eddie to get on with his work, Neil went into the house. The rest of the family were having breakfast around the big wooden table in the kitchen. Sam, Neil's black and white Border collie, and Sam's son, Jake, were both watching alertly, in the hope that someone might accidentally drop a sausage or a piece of toast.

"*Hurry up,* Neil," his mom said.

"Sorry," Neil said, giving his hands a quick wash. "I was talking to Eddie. He says everything's on time."

"Everything but your breakfast," said Carole.

Neil slid into his seat, poured cornflakes into his bowl, and splashed milk on top. "Dad, if Eddie's gutting the rescue center, where are you going to put the dogs?"

Bob Parker looked up from sorting the mail. "It's only a problem today. We're leaving the five pens down one side of the old center to use when it's a dog clinic, and there are only four rescue dogs at the moment."

"There are a couple of spare boarding pens," said Carole. "I'll have to juggle them around while the job's being done. But Eddie promised he'll be as quick as he can."

"Would you like me to stay at home and help?" Neil suggested. He met his mother's icy stare and wondered why she always insisted on putting school before dogs. "Just a thought."

He concentrated on gulping down cornflakes while Carole put sausage and bacon onto plates.

"There's a letter for you, Neil," said Bob.

Neil grabbed the envelope his father handed him. He recognized the black, squiggly handwriting. "Great, it's from Max!" Quickly, he tore the letter open and scanned the few lines inside. His face broke into a delighted grin. "He can come!"

Max Hooper, with his golden cocker spaniel, Prince, was the star of the Parkers' favorite TV show, *The Time Travelers.* He had become their friend when an episode was filmed at Padsham Castle, and so he was the obvious person to ask to come and open the new rescue center. Now it was even more important to have everything ready on time.

Emily had stopped with a piece of sausage half-way to her mouth. "That's awesome!"

"He says he can stay over Friday and Saturday night," said Neil.

"We've got to plan the day!" Emily announced, ruffling up her dark hair as she always did when she was excited. "It's got to be just right. We can have a pet show in the field, with prizes and races and invite everybody we know and —"

"And hope the weather stays nice," Bob finished for her, grinning.

"It's got to!" said Neil. "It wouldn't dare rain, not for our grand opening!"

By the time Neil got home from school, the Dumpster was full, although there was plenty of stuff still lying around. Neil left his bike beside the back door and went inside, calling for Jake. There would be just enough time before supper to give the young dog a training session.

The kitchen was empty of dogs and people. When Neil went into the hall, he heard his mother's voice coming from the office.

"Is that you, Neil? Jake's in the field with Emily." Carole appeared at the office door. "Charlie's out there as well. Will you ask Emily to bring him in? Linda Woodham, his owner, is coming to pick him up soon, and I want to give him a good brushing first."

"OK." Neil shot out of the back door again. As he hurried down the path, Sam appeared from underneath his favorite bush and trotted at Neil's side as far as the gate into the exercise field.

Neil leaned on the gate for a minute and watched Emily and Sarah running around with Jake and Charlie. Sarah was chasing the little golden retriever, shrieking with laughter, while Charlie bounced around as if he was laughing as well.

"He's a great little dog," Neil said, scratching Sam's head. "I'm glad he's coming back here soon."

He pushed open the gate and let Sam run ahead of him into the field. "Em!" he called. "Em, Mom wants you."

Emily came over to him. Her face was pink from running and her dark hair was sticking to her forehead. Jake was leaping beside her, trying to grab the stick she had been throwing for him.

"Jake, sit!" Neil said sternly.

Immediately, the young Border collie sat and looked alertly up at Neil. Neil slipped him a dog treat from the supply he always carried in his pocket and gave another to Sam, who was looking on hopefully.

"Jake's training is coming along really well," Emily said. "Are you going to give him a session now?"

"Yes, I want to practice the stay and recall commands. He keeps wanting to follow me the whole time." He grinned down at Jake. "But you'll get there, won't you, boy? You're going to be just as smart as your dad."

"What did Mom want me for?" Emily asked.

"She wants to spruce Charlie up before he's picked

up." He waved to Sarah, who was farther down the field with Charlie. "Hey, Squirt! Bring him over here!"

Sarah started to run back toward them, panting and laughing, with the cheerful little puppy still bounding around her feet.

"Can't Sarah take him in?" Emily asked. "I want to help you with Jake."

Neil shrugged. "I don't see why not. Squirt, can you take Charlie in to Mom? She has to get him ready to go home."

Sarah beamed with the importance of having a job to do. "Come on, Charlie. Heel!"

The little puppy was too young to know what "heel" meant, but he bounced off ahead of Sarah as she jogged back to the gate and up the path.

"OK," Neil said. "Now we can get down to business. Jake —" He broke off.

From the yard, where Sarah and Charlie had just disappeared, there came a joyful bark, followed by Sarah's voice shouting, "Charlie! Charlie!" Then her voice was drowned out by the sound of a truck.

Neil and Emily began to run for the gate. As they dashed through the yard, they saw the truck beginning to reverse through the gap in the fence to pick up the Dumpster, its reverse warning alarm adding to the racket.

Sarah was just ahead, crossing the yard at a stumbling run. At the other side, a tall, red-haired woman with an adult golden retriever on a leash had ap-

peared around the side of the house. Neil recognized
Linda Woodham and Charlie's mom, Tansy. Charlie
was shooting toward them, straight across the path
of the reversing truck.

Neil pushed Sarah aside and sprinted toward the
truck, knowing he was going to be too late. He yelled,
"Charlie! Charlie!" But the puppy just yapped excit-
edly, eager to greet his mom. Neil wanted to squeeze
his eyes shut so that he didn't have to watch.

Then, at the last second, Linda Woodham darted
forward, scooped Charlie up, and rolled over on the
ground with the little dog in her arms.

The truck driver must have seen Linda dash out
behind him. He stopped, turning off the engine. The
bleeping noise stopped. Tansy nosed up to Charlie,
who wriggled in his owner's grasp and licked his
mom's face.

The only sound that broke the silence was Sarah's
noisy sobbing.

Neil had stopped a few feet away from Linda and
her dogs. Emily came to join him, with a hand
through Jake's collar and Sam beside her. Carole,
white-faced, came out of the office and went over to
Linda. She held out a hand to help her up. "I'm so
sorry . . ." she began.

Linda Woodham looked up at her. Mud was smeared
down one side of her jeans and sweater and there
was mud on her face and hands. She looked upset
and furious all at once.

She ignored Carole's hand and scrambled to her feet, still clutching Charlie. "Mrs. Parker," she said icily, "maybe you can explain to me why trucks are moving around here without supervision, and why my dog is running loose with no one but a small child to look after him?"

Carole took a breath and began, "I . . ." She broke off and could find nothing else to say except to repeat, "I'm really sorry. It's just while we're building. . . ."

"At least Charlie's okay," Neil said.

Linda Woodham gave him an unfriendly look. "No thanks to you. Or to the rest of King Street Kennels. Mrs. Parker, I'm not satisfied with the service you're offering here. You haven't given nearly enough thought to safety."

As she gave her surroundings a chilly stare, Neil became acutely conscious of all that was still scattered around the site, the muddy ground, and the half-finished building.

"Nothing but the best is good enough for my dogs," Linda Woodham went on crisply. "You can cancel the rest of my bookings, Mrs. Parker. In the future I shall be taking Charlie elsewhere."

"Elsewhere?" Neil said indignantly.

"You haven't heard?" Linda Woodham's voice was cold. "There's a new dog kennel that just opened in Colshaw. I heard them advertising it on the local radio station, and they sound very professional."

"But you can't —" Neil began.

"Excuse me, I can do exactly what I like with my own dogs." Linda gave a last contemptuous glance at the untidy site. "Perhaps what you Parkers need is a bit of competition."

Still carrying Charlie, with Tansy trotting at heel, she turned her back and stalked off through the side gate.

CHAPTER TWO

When Linda Woodham left, the Parkers gathered in the kitchen, where Bob was peeling potatoes for dinner. Carole sat in the old basket chair by the window with Sarah on her lap; the five-year-old was still hiccuping with sobs.

"Dad, did you know about this new dog place?" Neil asked.

Bob paused with a potato in one hand and the peeler in the other. "It's called Pretty Paws," he explained. "It just opened in Colshaw. The man from Preston told me yesterday when he delivered the dog food."

"Oh, no!" said Emily.

"There used to be a kennel there years ago," Bob

went on. "It sounds as if somebody has opened it up again."

Neil kicked a chair and slumped down into it; for once nobody told him off. "Why would anybody want to go to a new kennel when we're here?"

Bob tried to grin though Neil could see he didn't feel like it. "Come on," he said. "Think of all the dogs in Compton and Colshaw and Padsham as well. There's more than enough room for another business. Your mother and I are always turning people away."

Neil grunted. "Bet they're not as good as King Street." He reached down to where Sam was sitting beside him and tickled the Border collie's ears. "Don't you think so, boy?"

"The Preston's man told me that Pretty Paws is a really fancy place," said Bob. "Silk cushions and three-course dinners."

Neil let out a snort of laughter. "You're putting me on! Nobody would put a dog on silk cushions. And if they did, who would choose them instead of King Street?"

Carole looked around from where she was cuddling Sarah. "Linda Woodham, for one."

As if she was reminded of that terrifying few seconds in the yard, Sarah started sobbing again. "Mommy, I couldn't help it! I was looking after Charlie — I was! But then he saw Tansy and ran away from me, and I couldn't catch him . . ." She buried her face in her mother's shoulder.

"It was my fault," Emily said quietly. "You told me to get Charlie, but I sent Sarah because I wanted to stay and help Neil."

"Now look." Bob turned away from the sink as he interrupted. "There's no point in saying it was anybody's fault. We were all careless, your mom and I included."

"We've got to realize we can't carry on like we used to," said Carole. "Not with all the building work going on."

"We were very lucky this afternoon," said Bob, "because nobody got hurt. We'll make sure nothing like that happens ever again."

"But Charlie won't be coming back." Sarah wept.

Carole hugged her. "No, dear, we've lost Charlie. And I can't say I blame Linda for being angry and taking him off to Pretty Paws."

"Pretty Paws!" Neil repeated. "What sort of name is that for a kennel? Who's running it anyway?"

Bob shrugged and went back to his peeling. "They're new to the area, the man from Preston's said. Just moved here from Manchester. Somebody named Sparrow."

"Sparrow!" Neil sat bolt upright. "Em, there's a couple of new kids at school named Sparrow."

Emily's eyes were wide open. "Yes, Toby Sparrow.

He's in my class. Nobody knows much about him yet."

"His sister's older." Neil sounded disgusted. "Amanda. She looks snooty. She's in Chris Wilson's class, thank goodness, not mine."

"You never know," said Carole. "They might be nice."

"Huh!" said Neil. "Pigs might fly."

As they climbed out of the green King Street Kennels Range Rover in front of the school the next morning, Emily grabbed Neil's arm. "There they are."

Neil looked where she was pointing. A tall, blond girl was standing in the middle of a group of kids, with a smaller boy beside her. Her voice was raised and Neil caught what she was saying as he drew closer.

". . . a real hotel, but for dogs. Each dog has its own little room, with curtains and a bed with cushions — pink silk cushions — and we bathe them with scented water, and they can choose what they want to eat, like chicken in cream sauce, and —"

"Just a minute," Neil interrupted as he made his way into the middle of the group. "You shouldn't feed dogs chicken in cream sauce, you know. It's bad for them."

Amanda Sparrow swung around to face Neil. Her

chilly blue eyes bored into him. "I know who you are," she said.

She was taller than Neil, which annoyed him to start with. Her hair was clipped back with glittery barrettes; Neil bet that Mr. Hamley, the principal, wouldn't let her wear those to school again. She had a thin face, and Neil thought she was looking down her nose at him.

Her brother, Toby, standing just behind her, was smaller and plumper, with brown hair and a faintly worried expression. He tugged his sister's arm. "Mandy —"

Amanda Sparrow shook him off and went on speaking to Neil. "You're Neil Parker. I've heard about you."

Neil didn't like her snooty voice any more than her stuck-up expression. "What have you heard?"

"I heard your family runs some sort of dog place."

"Some sort of dog place!" Suddenly Neil was so angry he could hardly speak. "We run King Street Kennels. We're the best!"

Amanda sniffed. "If you're so great, why did a dog nearly get run over when you should have been looking after him?"

"That's not —" Neil had started to protest before he realized that he couldn't excuse what had happened to Charlie. He fell silent. Glancing around, he realized that Chris and Hasheem had joined the group around them, along with Emily and her best friend, Julie. And Kathy Jones — who was the biggest gossip in the school. *Great!* Neil groaned to himself. *This story about Charlie is going to be all over Compton.* Weakly, he finished, "It was an accident. Anyone can have an accident."

Amanda Sparrow studied her fingernails. "Well, if *you've* been the best up till now," she said, "it's about time there was a decent place around here."

Neil took a deep breath, trying to keep his temper. The horrible Sparrows would just love it if he lost control.

"What are you doing in this school, anyway?" he asked. "I thought you lived in Colshaw?"

"Then you thought wrong. Pretty Paws is in Colshaw, but the apartment there isn't big enough for us. So Mom bought a house in Compton."

"But look," Neil said, suddenly becoming more worried than angry. "You can't leave dogs alone for the night. All kinds of things can happen . . ."

"I never said we left the dogs alone," Amanda replied. "That's all you know, Neil Parker. There's a kennel assistant who lives in the apartment. So there."

Neil still wasn't sure. Remembering all the hair-raising things that had happened at King Street, he knew that the best thing for boarding dogs was to have the people who ran the business on the site all the time. He couldn't imagine his mom and dad shutting the gate of the kennels at five o'clock and leaving the dogs behind.

"But what if —"

"You think you know everything about dogs, Neil Parker," said Amanda.

"He knows a lot," Julie Baker suddenly interrupted, loyally speaking up for Neil and King Street. "And his dad *does* know everything about dogs."

There was a murmur of agreement from the group around them. Neil suddenly felt encouraged and very proud of Bob. He could see that Emily was smiling.

"The Parkers have helped a lot of people around here," said Chris Wilson.

"And a lot of dogs," someone behind Neil added.

"So don't just walk in and start trashing them," Chris went on, beginning to sound angry.

"Yes," Hasheem agreed. "They're the Puppy Patrol. They belong here."

"And we don't?" Amanda snapped. She had gone pink, and Toby was looking even more worried. "We've got as much right to be here as they have."

"That's right," said Kathy Jones, unexpectedly joining in on Amanda's side. "You can't have it all your own way, Neil."

There were sounds of agreement to that, too — mostly, Neil noticed, from people who didn't own dogs.

Kathy tucked an arm through Amanda's. "Come on, I'll show you the school rabbits."

Amanda went with her, but as she turned away she glanced over her shoulder at Neil. "Charlie's coming to us now," she said. "And a lot of other dogs as well. If you're not careful, Neil Parker, there'll still be only one kennel around here, but it won't be King Street."

She tossed her head and walked off with Kathy. Toby glanced around uncertainly and then trailed after his sister with a miserable look on his face.

Neil's friends crowded around him. Chris slapped him on the shoulder. "Don't worry," he said. "Nobody will pay attention to her."

Neil wasn't sure his friend was right. What worried him was that far *too* many people might listen to what Amanda Sparrow said about King Street.

The bell rang for the start of morning classes. Neil thrust his hands in his pockets and shuffled his feet as he headed for the door.

Emily and Julie followed him. Just as they reached the steps, Julie burst into uncontrollable giggles.

"I'm glad someone feels cheerful," Neil muttered.

"Oh, I'm sorry, Neil," Julie gasped. "But I was just thinking about Ben. In a room with pink silk cushions . . . and a bath with scented water, and . . ."

She collapsed into giggles again, and this time a broad smile crept over Neil's face as well. Julie's Old English sheepdog was friendly and loving and the scruffiest dog alive. He could wreck a room within minutes; Neil's face lit up with laughter just thinking of what he might do to a pen at Pretty Paws. "I'd give anything to see that," he said.

"Well, you won't," Julie retorted. "We'd never send Ben anywhere except to King Street."

When Neil got out of school at the end of the day, he saw Bob Parker leaning against the Range Rover with a flyer in his hand. He held it out as Neil approached. "Look what I found under the windshield wiper."

Neil took the flyer. It was pale pink. At the top was the outline of a dog's paw, circled with fancy lettering: *Pretty Paws, for the dog with taste.*

Neil glanced at his dad, whose eyes were crinkled with amusement. He read on.

Does your doggy friend deserve the best? At Pretty Paws dog hotel you can choose from our gourmet menus — meals freshly prepared every day from the finest ingredients. Visit our grooming parlor where qualified staff will pamper your pet with shampoo and conditioner for the silkiest coat ever — finishing off with a splash of French perfume! See our full range of fashion coats and collars. Let your dog revel in the luxury of his own hotel room. Book before the end of the month and get an extra week absolutely FREE!

Then there was an address in Colshaw and a phone number.

Neil mimicked being sick and handed the flyer over to Emily, who had just appeared.

"Neil!" said Bob. "Don't be disgusting."

"It's that thing that's disgusting!" Neil retorted. "Perfume! Fashion collars! Who needs it?"

Emily laughed and gave the flyer back to her dad. "Nobody will take their dog there," she said. "It's silly."

"I don't know," said Neil. "It sounds like just the sort of place Mrs. Jepson would like for her dear little doggie-woggies."

"Not this time," said Bob. "Mr. and Mrs. Jepson have booked Sugar and Spice at King Street, starting Sunday."

"Oh, no!" said Emily, running her hands through her short dark hair. Nobody at King Street enjoyed looking after the spoiled little Westies.

"Oh, yes," said Bob. "And they're regular customers, whatever we might think about their doggie-woggies." He laughed, crumpled the flyer, and tossed it into the garbage by the school gate. "People will go on bringing their dogs to us because they know we offer real dog care," he said. "I don't think we need to worry about Pretty Paws."

CHAPTER THREE

"**D**ad, I've been thinking," Neil said when the Parker family had gathered around the kitchen table for dinner. "If the Sparrows are advertising Pretty Paws, maybe we should do something to publicize King Street."

Bob started to shake his head, but Carole said, "Neil's right. They've got a big advertisement in this week's *Compton News,* too. We know that King Street offers a much higher standard of dog care, but how will potential new customers know if we don't tell them?"

"Word of mouth has always been good enough for us," Bob said, digging a fork into his dinner. "Satisfied customers who tell their friends."

"But if Pretty Paws is advertising, we should, too," Emily protested.

"They'll just say we're copying them," said Neil. He grinned suddenly. "Unless we do something really original. Dad, you could walk around Compton town center with a poster saying 'Come to King Street'."

"Or get one of those planes," Emily said, her eyes lighting up. "You know, trailing a banner behind it . . ."

"Dad could parachute out of it," Neil suggested.

"Dressed up in a dog costume," Emily added, laughing. "Think what a picture that would make!"

Sarah giggled, swallowed a mouthful of orange juice the wrong way, and started choking.

"Now look what you've done," said Carole, patting her on the back. "Emily, get me some tissues."

While Sarah was being cleaned up, Neil chewed steadily through his dinner, thinking hard. "You know, Dad," he said at last, "we should do something different to advertise King Street, but — "

"You're not getting me in a dog suit," said Bob. "Or a parachute."

"No, listen, Dad. We should do something that shows how King Street is better for dogs — not for owners who want to make them into stupid toys."

Bob put down his knife and fork and looked at Neil. "Such as?" he asked.

"Well, what about your obedience classes? The Sparrows don't offer anything like that — they wouldn't know where to start. Why don't you give a special obedience class, free to anybody who has never boarded their dog with us before? Then they'd see how good you are with dogs."

"There could be something in that," Bob said thoughtfully, scratching his curly brown beard.

"We could combine it with a tour of the kennels," Carole suggested. "Give them a real taste of what King Street has to offer."

"And let's tell Linda Woodham about it," said Neil. "Maybe if she saw everything we can do, she would let Charlie come back."

Sarah bounced up and down in her seat. "Yes! I love Charlie."

"Well, I don't know about that," Bob said. "But the class is a good idea. We'll give it a try, OK?"

"Great!" said Emily. "When?"

"When we've had time to clean the place up a bit," said Carole.

"But soon," Neil insisted. "Or there's a chance that Pretty Paws will take all our customers."

Bob looked even more thoughtful as he cleared the plates and Carole brought fruit salad and yogurt to the table.

"Let's see," he said. "Today's Friday. I can get an ad into the *Compton News* for next Friday and an announcement on the local radio station."

"And I'll make a poster!" Sarah announced. "I'll draw the barn and all the dogs in the obedience class."

"Great, Squirt," Neil said, starting to feel excited.

"I bet Mike Turner will put it up in his waiting room." The Compton vet was always ready to help with whatever was going on at King Street. "And we can make some flyers on the computer."

"Then we could have the class next Saturday — a week from tomorrow," said Bob.

"That gives us a week to get the place looking tidier," said Carole. "And the new rescue center will start to look finished by then."

"Super!" said Neil. "We'll show the Sparrows what a real kennel is like. Eat your heart out, Pretty Paws!"

The next morning, Neil and Emily helped with the kennel work, and then, when Bob took Sarah to her ballet class, they decided to see what they could do to improve how the place looked. Neil got a garbage bag from the storeroom, and they started to fill it with all the smaller pieces of garbage that had failed to find their way into the Dumpster. Dust swirled up, stinging their eyes and making them cough.

"I don't know where it all comes from," Neil said, straightening up with half a soggy newspaper in his hand. He stuffed it into the bag. "My back's breaking. It's too bad we can't train Sam and Jake to pick it all up."

"They'd cut their paws," said Emily, showing Neil a piece of broken glass.

Carole had insisted that Sam and Jake should

stay in the house while Neil and Emily worked. The rule at King Street now was "no dogs running free." No one wanted to risk another scare like the one Charlie had given them.

Emily lifted the piece of glass very carefully in gloved hands and dropped it into the garbage bag. "We'll never —" she began and broke off at the sound of laughter coming from the old rescue center, along with a flurry of excited yapping.

Just outside the door, the workmen were sitting around on packing cases, drinking coffee. Neil turned to see what was going on. "Hey!" he said. "They've got a dog over there!"

Dropping the bag of trash, he walked over to have a closer look. The dog was a Pekingese, with a long, orange-colored coat. It was scratching vigorously at the knees of one of the builders, its eyes fixed on his cookie. The builder, a young man called Dan, was red with embarrassment.

"Get off, Pooh-Bah," he said. "You've had your breakfast. Get down, will you?"

Pooh-Bah the Pekingese took no notice. He managed to haul himself onto Dan's knee, panting with his pink tongue out and his black snub nose quivering.

"Oh, all right." Dan gave him the cookie. Pooh-Bah wolfed it down and nuzzled Dan affectionately. Dan scratched his ears and then snatched his hand away as one of the other men said, "I think he's got you where he wants you."

Horace, the man who had spoken, was old with white hair standing up in tufts around his ears. He was grinning widely as he watched Dan with the Peke. "You won't want to talk to us now," he said, "not with a fancy dog like that."

Neil squatted down beside Dan and tickled Pooh-Bah behind the ears. Pooh-Bah closed his eyes blissfully. "He's wonderful," Neil said to Dan. "Is he yours?"

Dan still looked embarrassed. He was a tall, hefty young man with close-cropped black hair. He and the silky Pekingese did look a bit strange together. "He was my grandmother's dog," he explained. "She died a couple of weeks ago and left him to me."

"He's a little overweight," Neil said, feeling the plump body under the flowing hair. "What are you feeding him?"

"Dog food," Dan said. "Out of a can."

"And cookies," said Neil.

Dan went red again. "He likes his cookies."

Neil sighed. "I'll get Dad to give you some information on diet for him."

"Well, I don't know . . ." Dan scratched the back of his neck and looked around uncomfortably at his coworkers. Horace was still grinning. Eddie Thomas smiled quietly into his mug of coffee, and the third, a thin, mousy-haired man named Mick, said, "That's a lady's dog, Dan. You can't walk through Compton with a dog like that."

"Why not?" Emily asked, reaching out so that Pooh-Bah could sniff her hand. "He's beautiful."

"Pekes are brave little dogs," said Neil. "The emperors of China used them as guard dogs."

Horace cackled with laughter. "Emperor Dan! How about that?"

"Be quiet," Dan muttered.

"Oh, I'm sorry, your Emperorship."

Neil thought Dan was starting to look really unhappy. "It's not going to work," the young man said. "I can't leave him at home all day. He yaps and howls when he's by himself, and the neighbors complain.

And when I bring him with me I get laughed at." He looked down at Pooh-Bah, who had draped himself contentedly over his knees and seemed to make his mind up. "Neil, your dad finds homes for dogs, doesn't he?"

"Well, yes, he does." Neil nodded toward the door of the rescue center. "There are four of them in there now, waiting for someone to come and take them."

"I got my Blackie from here," Eddie said.

"Well then . . ." Dan swallowed. "I think you'd better ask him to find another home for Pooh-Bah."

"Oh, no!" Emily exclaimed. "I mean, Dad will help, but are you sure that's what you want?" She stroked the Peke's long orange coat admiringly. "He seems so happy with you."

Dan shrugged. "We always got along, when I went to visit my granny. That's why she left him to me."

"Well, then . . ." said Neil.

As Dan hesitated, Emily added, "Don't decide now. Think about it."

"We'll have a word with Dad," Neil promised. "And there's a spare pen in the rescue center. You can put Pooh-Bah in there while you're at work, if it helps."

Dan looked relieved. "Thanks a lot. He does get under my feet. Granny never trained him to do as he's told."

Neil and Emily exchanged delighted grins. "You need the obedience class!" said Neil. He explained about the free class that was going to take place the

following week. "Should we put your name down?"
he asked Dan.

"Well . . . all right. But I still think he'd be better
off with somebody else."

Neil didn't try to argue but just said, "Put him in
the pen now, and we'll get him some water."

As he and Emily walked across the yard to get a
bowl of water from the storeroom, Neil glanced back
to see Dan coaxing Pooh-Bah into the rescue center.
The little Peke was bouncing around, tail waving
like a flag. The other builders still looked amused.

"They're stupid to laugh," Emily said, pink with
indignation. "They're spoiling everything for Dan. I
think he really likes Pooh-Bah."

"So do I. Still," Neil added, "if Dan comes to the
free class, he's got to keep Pooh-Bah for another
week. Maybe something will happen to make him
change his mind."

Neil dragged the third full bag of trash around to the
garage, ready for Bob Parker to load into the car and
take to the dump. He wiped one filthy hand over his
forehead.

"I'm finished!" he announced. "Come on, Em, let's
take Sam and Jake up on the ridge for an hour."

Emily wrapped a twist-tie around the neck of the
bag. "I'm all for that," she said. "Just as long as I
don't see any more trash!"

The two Border collies had been kept in the house,

except for a quick run in the exercise field earlier, so they were raring to go. Neil paused, panting, halfway up the slope to the top of the ridge, and watched Jake bounding on ahead of him.

"He's in better shape than you are," Emily said.

"He's hasn't been lugging bags around all day." He looked down at Sam, who was waiting for him to move on again. Recently, Sam had collapsed with a damaged heart, and Neil now had to be sure that he didn't overexert himself. "That's right, Sam," Neil went on. "Show Jake how —"

The noise of barking interrupted him. It was coming from the trail that ran along the top of the ridge.

"That's Jake!" said Neil. "What has he found?"

"Rabbits!" said Emily.

With Sam at heel, they hurried up the slope. Before they reached the top they could see a couple of people farther down the trail and hear the barking of another dog. Neil stopped. "Oh, no! Do you see what I see?"

Coming toward them through the brush were Amanda and Toby Sparrow. They had two dogs with them: a greyhound Neil had never seen before, and a small golden retriever puppy.

"It's Charlie!" exclaimed Emily.

Toby and Amanda also stopped when they saw Neil and Emily. Amanda said something to Toby; Neil was too far away to hear what it was. He would rather have turned around and gone another way,

but Jake was giving Charlie a friendly sniff and didn't come when Neil called to him. Neil walked up to him and snapped the leash on Jake's collar.

"Oh, it's the dog expert!" Amanda Sparrow said. "I thought dogs always did what you told them, Neil."

Neil felt himself going red. "Jake's too young," he said. "He's not properly trained yet." He couldn't help adding, "If you knew anything about dogs, you'd know that, too."

The greyhound, which was obviously well-trained, sat quietly beside Amanda while Charlie flopped down where he was standing. The little puppy looked exhausted. When Emily bent over him to say hello, he roused himself just enough to look at her and give her hand a lick.

"You haven't walked him all the way up from Colshaw, have you?" Neil asked.

"What if we have?" Amanda asked.

"But that's miles!" Neil gasped.

"We're helping," Toby added proudly. "Charlie's staying with us now."

"You're not helping if you make a little puppy like this walk all that way," Neil said. "Don't you know you could damage his growth? Twenty minutes a day is plenty for a dog of only four months old."

"He was loving it," Amanda said defensively. "He was jumping around all over the place."

Neil looked down at Charlie; the little dog was exhausted. "He isn't jumping around now. And anyway, that's not the point. A dog doesn't necessarily know what's best for him. It's up to his owners to know for him."

"You'll have to carry him back," Emily said. "He'll never make it on his own."

"Carry him!" Amanda's voice rose. "I'm not carrying him all that way."

"I will." Toby scooped up Charlie in his arms and cuddled him against one shoulder. "Come on, Charlie."

He turned and plodded off down the trail in the direction they had come. Amanda, looking suddenly furious, jerked the greyhound's leash and flounced off after him.

"Don't pull her like that!" Neil called after her.

Amanda ignored him.

Emily was watching the retreating Sparrows. "Toby's not so bad," she said thoughtfully.

"Maybe," Neil agreed. "But just keep his snooty sister away from me!"

CHAPTER FOUR

"**Y**ou know what bothers me most about Pretty Paws," said Neil.

"No, what?" Emily asked. After dinner she had spread her books out on the kitchen table and was struggling with her math homework.

Neil was managing quite successfully not to think about his own homework. "It's that the Sparrows don't live there. What happens if anything goes wrong at night?"

"Amanda says they've got a kennel assistant," Emily said, counting on her fingers.

Neil snorted. "Would you be happy if it was just Kate here at night by herself?"

Emily slowly shook her head. Kate McGuire loved dogs, and she was almost as good with them as Bob

Parker himself, but in a real emergency one person alone wasn't enough.

"Remember that night the barn caught fire?" Neil said.

Emily didn't need to answer. None of the Parkers would ever forget that night. It had taken a team effort by all of them, even Sarah, to deal with the flames and the frightened dogs.

"What do you think we should do, then?" Emily asked.

"I want to go and have a look at Pretty Paws."

Emily stared at him. "Neil Parker, that is absolutely the craziest idea I've ever heard. If the Sparrows catch us there, we're dead." Then she grinned. "Let's do it."

Neil sat down at the table and leaned forward, pushing Emily's math books aside. "Listen. It's Saturday evening. They don't live on site, so they won't be there now. We've got just enough time to bike over to Colshaw, scope the place out, and be back before lights out."

"Mom and Dad will want to know where we're going," Emily pointed out.

"No problem. We'll say we're taking Sam for a walk. We just won't say where."

At the mention of a walk, Sam got up from his basket and barked eagerly.

"All right," said Emily. "And what then?"

Neil shrugged. "If it's okay, then nobody will ever

know. If there's a real problem, I'll tell Dad. If the dogs at Pretty Paws aren't being properly looked after, he'll find some way of helping them."

Neil and Emily leaned their bikes against the red brick wall that surrounded Pretty Paws, in a quiet road on the outskirts of Colshaw. A few yards farther along was an archway with a wrought-iron gate. At the top of the arch was a sign, painted pink, with the same dog's paw logo as on the flyer, and the words *Pretty Paws Dog Hotel.*

Sam trotted up to the gate. Cautiously, Neil and Emily followed and peered through the wrought-iron lattice. In front of them was a cobblestone courtyard. To the right and left were long kennel blocks. Immediately opposite was a two-story building like an old-fashioned stable with a clock tower and an arched passageway leading through the middle. Pigeons cooed and fluttered on the roof. In the center of the courtyard was a bed of flowering shrubs. Everything was neat and clean, and the white paintwork shone.

"It's nice!" said Emily, sounding dismayed.

Neil was impressed, too, especially when he remembered the sea of mud and garbage around the new building at King Street, but he wasn't going to admit it. "It's what goes on here that matters," he said.

Without much hope, he tried the gate and was surprised when it swung open. He slipped warily inside, with Sam at his heels and Emily just behind. They were both prepared for someone to call out or come to see who they were, but no one appeared as they advanced into the courtyard.

"You couldn't do this at King Street," Neil said, cheering up at the thought that Pretty Paws wasn't perfect. "Walking in like this — we could be anybody. Let's look here first," he added, pointing to the building opposite. "If we go into the kennel blocks we'll set all the dogs off. Sam, you keep quiet."

Sam, panting cheerfully, looked up at Neil as if he understood.

Emily had crossed the courtyard and was peering in at the end window. "This is the office."

Looking over her shoulder, Neil saw a desk with a computer and telephone, filing cabinets and shelves. It looked tidy and well-organized, but not particularly interesting. Neil moved on to the next window, and let out a long whistle. "Here, Em — come and look at this."

Emily joined him and pressed her nose against the glass. After a few seconds, she giggled. "I don't believe it!"

Neil thought that he was looking at a hairdressing salon, rather than somewhere you might take a dog.

"Look!" said Emily. "Those are cans of hairspray! And jars of bath salts! And I bet those little glass bottles have perfume in them."

"And over there in those trays," Neil pointed out. "Hair curlers! Hey, Sam, do you think you'd look good with curlers in?"

Sam had reared up on his hind legs and set his front paws on the windowsill so he could look in, too. At Neil's question he gave a disapproving bark. Neil laughed and rumpled his ears. "Don't worry, boy. I wouldn't do it to you."

Emily ran across the arched opening to the window of the first room on the other side. Neil tore his eyes away from the grooming parlor and went to see what else she had found.

This next room was the reception area. There were comfortable chairs, a coffeemaker, and racks of dog magazines. On one wall was a display of fancy coats and collars.

"And dog booties!" Emily said, doubling over with laughter. "Oh, look Neil, aren't they sweet? Can't you just see Julie's Ben in those?"

But somehow Neil had stopped feeling it was funny. Any dog who came here would go away again looking completely stupid. It wasn't fair. Dogs were dogs, not silly toys for owners with more money than sense. Curling and scenting a dog and dressing it up was maybe not as bad as a beating or neglect, but it still wasn't right.

"Let's go," he said. "I've seen enough."

Before Emily could reply, there came the sound of a door opening, and a voice said, "Hello. Can I help you?"

Neil swung around. A girl had appeared in the courtyard. She was tall and slim, with a short, tight skirt and a pink T-shirt with the Pretty Paws logo emblazoned across it. Her blond hair was fluffed out like a chrysanthemum with pink streaks at the front. Her fingernails and toenails were painted pink and she wore high-heeled pink sandals.

"Hello," she repeated. "I'm Pauline — the kennel assistant. Can I help you?"

Neil became aware that he was gaping. He shut his mouth, grabbed frantically for something to say, and began, "Er . . . hello. We —"

"Have you come to book in your sweet little doggy?"

The girl tottered across the courtyard in her tall shoes and bent down to pat Sam. Sam shied away. Neil wasn't sure whether it was the shock of being called a sweet little doggy or the powerful whiff of perfume that came from Pauline.

"Don't be frightened, little doggy," she said. "I won't hurt you."

Neil started to boil with indignation at the way she was speaking to his dog. He still couldn't find anything sensible to say, but Pauline didn't seem bothered.

"Do you want to look around?" she asked. "I'm sure you'll like what you see, and then your mommy and daddy can come and make the booking."

Neil and Emily exchanged a glance. Pauline had obviously assumed they were there because they wanted to board Sam, and Neil didn't see any reason to tell her different.

"Yes, please," he said and kicked Emily on the ankle as she added, "Our little doggy would like to see everything."

Pauline led the way to one of the kennel blocks. When she opened the door, Neil could see a passage running between two rows of pens, much like the kennel blocks at King Street. Unlike King Street, the lighting was low and tinted pink, and there was a tinkle of music coming from somewhere.

"These are our doggy suites," said Pauline. "We aim for a very high standard of comfort for your dog, with no expense spared."

Neil and Emily peered into the first pen. Emily gasped. "Look, there's Charlie!"

The little golden retriever was sprawled on pink cushions piled up in a basket. But it wasn't the magnificence of the pen that caught Neil's attention. It was the way the pup looked so exhausted, lying with eyes half-closed, not even noticing them. Neil remembered the bright, bouncing little dog at King Street, and he began to feel angry.

"He looks worn out," Emily said.

"Yes, he had a really long walk today." Pauline was smiling. "We give all the dogs lots of exercise."

Even when they don't need it, Neil thought. *This woman knows nothing about dogs! What sort of kennel assistant is she?*

"Have you been a kennel assistant long?" he asked.

"Oh, no." Pauline laughed. "Only a month. I was a hairdresser before that. I do love grooming the dear little doggies." She turned away from Charlie's pen and led the way out of the kennel block again. "Come on, I'll show you where I work."

But as they started to cross the courtyard again, there was the sound of a car door closing in the road outside. A woman opened the wrought-iron gate and came in. She said, "Oh, Pauline, I just dropped in to get —"

Neil scarcely saw the woman because he was staring at the girl and boy who were following her into the courtyard.

Amanda and Toby Sparrow.

"Uh-oh," said Emily.

"Mom!" Amanda loudly interrupted what her mother was saying. "Mom, that's Neil and Emily Parker! It's those horrible kids from King Street Kennels!"

CHAPTER FIVE

Mrs. Sparrow took a few steps forward. She was small, with wispy blond hair and the same thin face as Amanda. "Is that true?" she asked.

"Yes," said Neil. "We —"

"Then what are you doing here? We're not open to visitors after six."

"They're spies!" Amanda said spitefully. "Throw them out, Mom."

"They said we don't know how to look after dogs," Toby added.

His mother glanced at him and back to Neil. "I'd like an explanation, please."

Neil swallowed. He hadn't thought about what he was going to say if the Sparrows caught him. "Well, we came to see —"

This time it was Pauline who interrupted. "They said they wanted to board their dog."

"We did not!" Emily exclaimed.

Mrs. Sparrow ignored her. "Pauline, these two are from King Street Kennels in Compton. They're the last people who would want to board a dog with us." To Neil and Emily she added, "You shouldn't be here, and you certainly shouldn't be telling lies about it. Will you go now, please."

"We haven't been telling lies," Neil protested, feeling a bit guilty.

Mrs. Sparrow said nothing. She just stood waiting for him and Emily to leave. There was nothing for Neil to do but call Sam and head for the gate. A wave of heat — mixed with fury and embarrassment — swept over him as he walked past Amanda Sparrow and saw the satisfied smirk on her face.

"I'll say this for you, Neil," said Bob Parker, "when you do something stupid, you *really* do something stupid."

"I did it, too." Emily defended her brother.

"But I bet I know whose idea it was."

Neil and Emily had arrived home to discover that Mrs. Sparrow had called their parents with a long complaint about their behavior. Bob and Carole had asked for their side of the story while they drank hot chocolate in the kitchen.

"You see, Neil," Bob went on, "we can be business

rivals with Pretty Paws without being enemies. At least we could have been, before tonight."

"But Dad, we had to do it," Neil said. "I'm worried about the dogs. There's nobody there at night except Pauline, and she's a complete airhead!"

"And what are we supposed to do about it?" Carole asked. "Mrs. Sparrow must have been inspected by the council before they allowed her to open."

"Well, I don't know," said Neil. "But I didn't think you'd just ignore it if there are dogs in trouble!"

"No one's ignoring it," said Bob. "And I'm not happy with what you've told me about Charlie. But they're not our dogs, and Pretty Paws isn't our property. There's nothing we can do."

"There must be!" Emily protested. "We could tell Linda Woodham."

"No!" Carole said sharply. "At least let your dad and me talk about it. You and Neil say nothing to anybody about Pretty Paws. You could get yourself into all sorts of trouble. Mrs. Sparrow is angry enough with you as it is."

"We didn't tell lies . . . not really," muttered Emily.

"Well, you certainly didn't tell the truth!" Carole snapped. Neil felt like hiding under the table.

"All the same," Bob said calmly, "Pretty Paws is out of bounds from now on. Unless the Sparrows invite you there, of course."

"That's *so* likely!" said Emily.

"I wouldn't go if they did," said Neil. "The farther I stay away from those Sparrows, the better!"

Neil was in the kitchen plodding through his history homework the following afternoon when Carole came in from the office.

"I've just seen the Jepsons' car pulling up," she said. "Will you come and give me a hand with Sugar and Spice?"

Neil threw his pen down reluctantly. Normally he would have been delighted to leave his homework to help with dogs, but even history looked better when the other option was Sugar and Spice. The two Westies were undoubtedly the Parkers' worst boarders ever.

He followed his mom outside to where Mr. Jepson and his wife were getting out of the car.

"Good afternoon," said Carole. "Everything's ready. If you'll give me the vaccination certificates, Neil and I will take Sugar and Spice to their pen."

Mrs. Jepson smoothed down her bright blue dress. It was far too tight for her, with ruffles around the neck and sleeves. Her dyed blond hair was pinned up on top of her head, and she wore enormous dangly earrings.

"Oh, but Mrs. Parker . . ." she began.

"We're not leaving Sugar and Spice with you," Mr. Jepson said flatly. He was a tall, bony man with a gloomy face.

"What do you mean?" asked Carole.

Shrill barking from the Westies interrupted Mr. Jepson's reply. They were scratching at the car door with their faces pushed against the glass. Both wore bows in their hair — blue for Spice, pink for Sugar — with matching collars studded with shiny stones.

Spice scrambled into the front of the car and launched himself at Mrs. Jepson, who scooped him up and planted a kiss on the end of his nose. "There's my sweetie-pie!"

When Mr. Jepson could make himself heard again, he began uncomfortably, "My wife feels —"

"You'll understand, Mrs. Parker," Mrs. Jepson said, her voice oozing false sweetness. "I've got to have the best for my little doggie-woggies."

Evenly, Carole said, "Up until now you seemed to think you *were* getting the best at King Street."

Mrs. Jepson gave a long sigh. "Yes, but you're so unkind to my darlings. They don't get any treats here, and they do love them so!"

Neil suddenly understood. He opened his mouth, only to close it again at a warning glance from Carole. He was not at all surprised when Mrs. Jepson said, "So we decided that the little dears would be happier at Pretty Paws."

"Really?" said Carole. Her voice was quiet, but when she used that particular tone Neil knew it was best to head for cover. "You have a booking with us, you know. We won't be able to fill that pen at such short notice."

Mr. Jepson frowned. "Are you saying we can't do what we think best for our own dogs?"

"What's the problem?" Bob Parker's voice broke in as he appeared through the gap in the fence. "Hello Mr. Jepson, Mrs. Jepson. Come to leave the Terrible Two with us?"

Mrs. Jepson looked indignant. Carole quickly explained to Bob that the Jepsons had decided to take Sugar and Spice to Pretty Paws instead.

Bob stroked his beard thoughtfully. "Well, if that's what you want. . . . But you know, Mr. Jepson, Mike Turner told you quite clearly that it's not good for the dogs to be given their own way all the time."

"You would say that," Mr. Jepson pointed out, "seeing as you want the dogs to come here."

Neil thought he was going to boil over. How dare Mr. Jepson suggest that Bob was only interested in their boarding fees!

"You're going to have a lovely shampoo and set, aren't you, my baby?" Mrs. Jepson cooed, cuddling Spice up to her face. Spice swiped her with one paw and brought half her hair tumbling out of its pins.

"Well," said Bob, "of course we have to respect your decision."

"But you do realize," Carole added, "that we can't refund your deposit?"

Mr. Jepson looked as if he was going to argue, thought better of it, and got back into the car. Mrs. Jepson put Spice into the back, managed to stop Sugar from diving out while the door was open, and got in beside her husband. The three Parkers watched as the Jepsons' car disappeared down the drive.

"Huh!" Neil was almost relieved to see them go. "We'll be better off without them. Let somebody else listen to them barking at all hours."

"That's all very well, Neil," his mother said. "But when we lose a customer, we lose their boarding fees as well. Sugar and Spice have been regular visitors."

Bob Parker tugged his beard; he was looking worried. "I really felt I was making some progress with those dogs — and with their owners. If they go to Pretty Paws, they'll be right back where they started."

"Em, have you got the flyers?"

Emily patted her schoolbag. "In here."

On Monday night, Neil and Emily had designed flyers on the office computer to advertise King Street Kennels and Bob's free obedience class. Now, after school on Tuesday, they were on their way into Compton to hand them out.

Neil was proud of those flyers. Instead of stupid collars and cushions, they described all the good things that King Street offered dogs, like the experienced staff and the regular visits from Mike Turner to check the dogs' health. They even previewed the opening of the new on-site dog clinic.

As Neil and Emily wheeled their bikes around the corner of the school building, they saw a little knot of people beside the gates.

"It's those Sparrows again," said Neil. "What are they doing now?"

"Who cares?" said Emily.

Laughter was coming from the group and the sound of high-pitched barking. As they drew closer, Neil could see that Amanda Sparrow had a small, gray poodle in her arms. He stopped and stared.

"Em, that's Sheba!" He reached out and grabbed

his sister's arm. "It's Mrs. Fitz's Sheba!" The perky poodle was another regular boarder at King Street Kennels and it came as a surprise to both of them to see her with the Sparrows.

Emily frowned. "Why is she with them?"

"Dunno. Unless —" Neil broke off as an awful possibility hit him. "Unless . . . Oh, no. Mrs. Fitz is sending Sheba to Pretty Paws!"

CHAPTER SIX

Toby Sparrow scratched the gray curls on Sheba's head and held out a piece of chocolate in front of her nose. Sheba strained toward it, panting eagerly. Toby popped it into her mouth. The little poodle wolfed it down and looked for more. The children around her laughed, admiring her and petting her.

Neil dropped his bike, walked over to the gate and gently said to Toby, "You really shouldn't be giving her chocolate. It's bad for her."

"Oh, no, it's Neil know-it-all Parker!" Amanda butted in. "What gives you the right to interfere?"

"I'll interfere if I see a dog being ill-treated," Neil retorted.

"We're not ill-treating her," Toby said. "She loves chocolate. Look."

He gave Sheba another piece. Neil could see the brown sticky stuff smeared all over the little dog's teeth."

"That's not the point," Neil explained. "It's bad for her teeth, and if she has too much she'll get fat. If you want to give a dog a treat, you get special biscuits like these." He pulled a handful of dog treats out of his pocket and gave one to Sheba. "They like these just as much, and they're the right kind of food for a dog."

"What are you doing with Sheba anyway?" Emily asked, coming up beside Neil. "Julie, do you know anything about this?"

Julie Baker was standing in the group around the Sparrows. She lived next door to Sheba's owner, Mrs. Fitzherbert.

She shook her head. "I know Mrs. Fitz is going to visit her daughter. But I thought she was taking Sheba with her."

"Then you thought wrong," Amanda said in a nasty, sneering voice. "Mrs. Fitz's daughter has a new baby, and she doesn't think she can cope with a dog in the house as well. So Sheba's coming to stay with us at Pretty Paws."

"But . . ." Neil just stood with his mouth open. He hadn't really believed it until Amanda told him. Losing Sugar and Spice had been one thing, but he had thought that Mrs. Fitz was a friend.

"Mom just picked up Sheba," Toby explained proudly. "Mrs. Fitz doesn't have her own car."

He obviously had no idea that Pretty Paws had just stolen a customer from King Street, but Amanda understood the shock in Neil's face.

"Don't think that everybody has to come to King Street," she said. "You precious Parkers think you own every dog in Compton."

"Listen," said Julie furiously. "That dog you've got there wouldn't even be alive if it wasn't for the Parkers — and my dog Ben. What have you ever done for Sheba?"

"We're going to look after her now," said Amanda. She kissed the little poodle on the top of her head. "We promised Mrs. Fitz we'd make her look really beautiful for when she comes home."

"Huh! Perfume and ribbons!" Neil snorted.

"And what's wrong with that?"

Neil exchanged a glance with Emily. He could have spent a week telling Amanda what was wrong with that, but she wouldn't have listened.

"Maybe you need one of these." Emily pulled out a flyer from her schoolbag and held it out to Amanda. "Find out the right way to look after dogs."

Amanda turned her nose up, but Toby took the flyer and pored over it. Neil saw his eyes widen as he read about all that King Street had to offer. He was finding out for the first time that there was more to dog care than chocolate.

A car horn tooted. Amanda pulled Toby's sleeve. "Mom wants us."

Neil saw a pink minivan parked a few feet down the road from the school gates. It had the Pretty Paws logo on the door, and Mrs. Sparrow was at the wheel. Amanda waved and called, "Coming!" To Neil and Emily she said, "You just wait. Everybody will bring their dogs to Pretty Paws before long."

She flounced off, still cuddling Sheba. Toby met the stares of Neil, Emily, and Julie, and followed his sister. Neil saw that he pushed the flyer into his pocket as he went.

"Well!" said Julie. "I never would have thought Mrs. Fitz would do that!"

"Remember how she used to spoil Sheba?" Neil said. "And how nervous Sheba used to be? I bet the Sparrows are just encouraging her to be fussy again." He remembered what his dad had said about Sugar and Spice. "Sheba will just go right back to where she started. It's hopeless."

Neil didn't feel like talking while he and Emily biked into the center of Compton. It wasn't just that Pretty Paws was taking business away from King Street. The Sparrows were *mistreating* the dogs as well. Dogs that Bob Parker had worked with and done his best for were going to slip back into all their old bad habits. And it wasn't the dogs' fault, Neil reflected. Every dog deserved proper care and training — even Sugar and Spice.

Neil and Emily got off their bikes in Compton's

market square, where a statue of Queen Victoria looked disapprovingly down her nose at the public library.

While they were locking the bikes to the Queen's railings, Emily said, "Come on, Neil. It's not that bad."

"The Sparrows don't know how to treat dogs," Neil grunted. "And there's nothing we can do about it!"

"Yes, there is." Emily's tone was bracing. "We can hand out these flyers and tell people where the real dog care is around here."

Neil gazed at his sister and reluctantly started to grin. "You're right, Em," he said. "Let's go for it!"

They walked down the street from the market square, past the parish church in the direction of the park. Whenever they saw someone with a dog, they handed them a flyer. Most of the owners smiled and said thank you and looked interested. One of them, an elderly man with a Jack Russell terrier that was pulling obstinately at the leash, chuckled and said, "Obedience, eh? I'll give your dad a call as soon as I get home!"

Neil was feeling much better by the time they reached the park. He and Emily had handed out almost all their flyers when they saw a tall, red-haired woman sitting on a bench with a beautiful adult golden retriever at her feet, and a young pup playing happily on the grass nearby.

"It's Linda Woodham!" said Emily. "With Tansy

and Charlie." She looked at the last few flyers in her hand. "Do we dare to?"

"Why not?" said Neil. "She can only say no."

Boldly, he walked over to the bench. "Hello, Mrs. Woodham. You've got Charlie back home again."

Linda Woodham looked slightly surprised, then she smiled and said, "Hello, Neil. Yes, I picked him up from Pretty Paws yesterday."

"And was he all right?" Neil couldn't resist asking.

"He seemed a bit quiet at first, but he's fine now."

Neil was tempted to tell Linda how Amanda and Toby had given Charlie too much exercise, but he remembered what his dad had said and kept quiet.

Emily sat on the grass and held out her arms to Charlie, who hurtled toward her and flung himself on top of her, paws flying, one ear folded comically back over his head.

Linda started to look more friendly. "He remembers you."

"I think he's adorable." Emily stroked Charlie's thick, fluffy coat admiringly. "His fur's so soft and creamy."

"He'll get darker soon," said Linda. "More the color of his mom. Look at the tips of his ears. That's the color he'll be when he's fully grown."

Emily traced the edge of Charlie's ear with one finger. "Shiny gold. Gorgeous!"

"Did Tansy do well at the shows?" Neil asked.

"Yes . . . she won her class."

"That's great!" Neil thought Linda Woodham didn't look quite as pleased as he would have expected.

"It's not as good as I'd hoped," Linda explained. "I wanted her to be Best in Show. You see, if she wins three Challenge Certificates for being Best in Show, under three different judges, then she's a Show Champion, and there aren't very many of those. She already has two." She patted Tansy and ran her hand over the dog's strong neck and shoulders. "You're a beautiful girl, aren't you?" To Neil she added, "If she can win her third certificate soon, I'll retire her from showing and use her for breeding."

"And bring Charlie on as a show dog?" Neil asked.

"That's right. That's why Charlie is spending so much time in kennels lately. There's another show next week, so he'll have to go in again."

Neil didn't dare ask Linda outright whether she would consider sending Charlie back to King Street, but he handed her a flyer. While she was reading it he couldn't help thinking it was a bit forward suggesting an obedience class to her, when Tansy was so perfectly trained.

"It sounds interesting," Linda said at last. "But I'm not sure I need a class, and anyway I'm not entitled to the free one. I've already used King Street."

She started to hand the flyer back. Neil said, "You could come and watch if you like, to see what we do."

"Well . . ." Linda paused. "Thank you, Neil. I might just do that."

"And we could still put Charlie in the class," Emily suggested. "I'm sure Dad wouldn't mind."

Charlie gave a little bark, as if he was agreeing. Linda laughed. "He knows what he wants." She tucked the flyer into her pocket. "I'll check my schedule, and if we're free I'll call your dad and ask him if it's OK to come."

"Well," said Bob Parker, smiling broadly as he came into the kitchen next Saturday afternoon, "that's another job done."

Neil and Emily and Sarah were clustered together

at the kitchen table with their heads together over a piece of paper. Neil looked up. "What job is that?"

"I've been on the phone with Daltons, the landscape gardeners. They're going to plant some flowers and lay turf around the new rescue center before the grand opening next week."

"Won't that be expensive?" Carole had the *Compton News* spread out on the table, looking at the advertisement for their opening. "Can we afford it?"

"I think so," said Bob. "Think of it as an investment. If the people who come to the opening see the place looking attractive, they're more likely to use us in the future."

"True," said Carole.

"Look at this, Dad." Emily waved the piece of paper in front of her father. "We've been planning the pet show for next week."

Bob took the paper and read aloud: *"Class Number One: the dog with the waggiest tail. Number Two: the pet most like its owner. Number Three: the pet the judge would most like to take home.* Who's going to judge this?" he asked. "I hope you're not going to ask me. I'll get lynched."

"Already done," said Emily. "I asked Mike Turner, Terri McCall, and Gavin Thorpe."

Bob frowned. "I can understand a vet and the SPCA officer," he said, "but why have you asked the vicar? Gavin knew next to nothing about dogs until he got Jet."

"But he's the pastor," Emily said, grinning. "Do you think anybody will dare to argue with him?"

Bob laughed. "It's going to be great," he said. "But have a couple of more serious classes, too. The healthiest pet, say, or the best groomed."

Emily started scribbling.

"I'm going to enter Fudge," said Sarah. She thought her hamster was the best pet in the world.

"What as?" asked Neil. "The pet most likely to give the judge a nervous breakdown?"

Sarah fell on him and started to tickle him. Neil fended her off. Jake caught the excitement and ran around the kitchen, barking.

"When you've all finished," Carole said, "I hope you haven't forgotten that the free obedience class is due to start in ten minutes."

"It's all organized," Bob said calmly. "Neil and Emily swept the barn out first thing this morning."

"Good," said Carole. "I'll show the owners around afterward and answer any questions. And just remember, everybody. King Street Kennels is on show. It's very important to get it right."

Everyone nodded seriously.

"How many people are coming?" Neil asked.

"Eleven," said Bob. "That's including Dan and Pooh-Bah, but not counting Linda Woodham. There's not much anyone can teach her about dog training, but she's coming to watch."

"Can I bring Jake?"

"Glad to have you," Bob said. "And maybe Emily would like to take Charlie in?"

"Great!" said Emily, her eyes shining.

The doorbell rang.

"This is it!" said Bob, rubbing his hands together. "Puppy Patrol, forward march!"

CHAPTER SEVEN

Eleven rather nervous owners stood around inside the barn while their dogs pulled away from them and tried to investigate one another. Among them were the young builder, Dan, with Pooh-Bah, and Mr. Smith, the old man Neil and Emily had met in Compton, with his Jack Russell terrier, Bobby.

Linda Woodham was sitting on a bale of straw near the door of the barn, with Tansy at her feet. She had handed Charlie over to Emily, who was standing in line with the other dogs, beaming with pleasure at being in charge of the little golden retriever.

Neil tacked on to one end of the line with Jake, while Bob welcomed the owners to King Street and launched into his poop-scoop lecture about always cleaning up after their dogs.

Neil noticed that the Basset hound at the other end of the line was whining and straining toward the bales of straw that were stacked against the far wall of the barn. Neil wondered what was so interesting. *I hope we don't have rats,* he thought, *not on top of all our other problems.*

"Okay," said Bob. "First we'll get your dogs to heel. Would you all walk around the barn, please. Neil, lead the way."

Neil set off with Jake trotting at his heel. The young Border collie had learned to do this quite recently, and Neil was proud of him.

Charlie started by trying to bite his own tail, but Emily soon managed to get him under control. Bobby was pulling ahead as he had done on the street, and Pooh-Bah started running around Dan in small circles, so that after a few steps Dan had to stop and unwind the leash from around his ankles. He was blushing furiously.

"Shorten the leash," Bob advised him calmly. "And if he tries to pull away, give it a gentle tug."

Dan got going again, and this time the Peke trotted along close beside him. *Good,* thought Neil. *If Pooh-Bah makes progress, maybe Dan will want to keep him after all.*

"Great," said Bob after the exercise had continued for a few more minutes. "Now, let me see you all praising your dogs so that they'll want to try again next time."

Neil squatted down beside Jake, patted him, and slipped him a tidbit from the supply in his pocket. The young dog looked happy and alert.

"That's good," said Bob. "Now, we'll go on with the command to sit. When you give a command to your dog, you —"

Whatever Bob had been about to say was drowned out by a spate of furious barking from the basset hound, joined almost at once by Bobby, the Jack Russell, and a Staffordshire bull terrier. Heads swiveled to look at the stack of bales at the end of the barn.

Neil groaned aloud.

Standing on top of the bales, with back arched and tail fluffed out, was an enormous black cat.

Bob Parker was the first person to move, striding swiftly down the length of the barn. "Hang on to your dogs!" he called.

Too late. The basset hound was already pawing at the foot of the stack of bales, tugging on his fully extended leash, trying to climb up to the cat. Mr. Smith was struggling to hang on to Bobby. The Staffie's teeth were bared in a fierce growl. A little black Scottie was lunging back and forth on the end of her leash, her barking adding to the general din, and Pooh-Bah, yipping in a frenzy, had reared up on his hind feet in his efforts to get away from Dan.

Linda Woodham still had Tansy under control, but Charlie, terrified by the noise, had flattened himself on the ground and paid no attention to Emily when she stroked him and tried to reassure him. Linda went over to her and said something Neil could not hear because of the racket the other dogs were making.

Neil gave Jake the *sit* command. The Border collie obeyed, but Neil couldn't leave him to go and help Bob. His dad jumped up onto one of the lower bales and reached for the cat, but the cat leaped to his shoulder, then to the bale he was standing on, then to the floor, and shot out of the half-open barn door. Pooh-Bah pulled the leash away from Dan and launched himself in hot pursuit.

"Pooh-Bah! Come back!" Dan bellowed, but the Peke took no notice.

"C'mon, Jake!" Neil hurried after them and was in time to see the cat run across the open ground, past the kennel blocks in the direction of the yard. Pooh-Bah, trailing his leash, bounded along after it, still yapping frantically.

As Neil pounded along in their wake, Carole appeared from the house and stared in bewilderment. "What —"

Neil pushed Jake's leash into her hand. "Cat. Can't stop now."

When he caught up with Pooh-Bah, the Peke was sitting at the foot of the horse chestnut tree at the far end of the yard. The cat was just visible on one of the lower branches, peering balefully through the leaves.

Neil grabbed the end of the Peke's leash and gave it a tug. "Heel, Pooh-Bah."

The Peke didn't want to give up. Neil guessed the little dog hadn't had so much fun in ages. He might have laughed, if his father's special class hadn't been so disastrously broken up.

He eventually got the Peke under control and, leaving the cat to look after itself, he went back to the barn.

All the owners and their dogs were standing around outside. Bob was dabbing his face with a handkerchief. Neil could see a red streak where the cat had scratched him.

As Neil came up to his father he heard the Scottie's owner say, "Well, if this is an obedience class, I don't think much of it." He walked away, pulling his dog after him. The woman with the basset hound followed without saying anything. Neil watched helplessly. There wasn't anything he could do to make them stay.

"This is a catastrophe!" said Bob.

The Staffie's owner paused beside him. "Mr. Parker," she said. "I've spent a lot of time and effort trying to keep my dog away from cats. I didn't expect you to make the problem worse."

She left as well, along with the other owners and their dogs. Dan came hurrying up to take Pooh-Bah and led the little Peke away toward the rescue center without saying anything.

Neil looked around for Linda Woodham. She was squatting on the ground near the barn door, cuddling Charlie in her arms. Charlie was shivering and hiding his head. Emily, beside her, looked close to tears.

Neil felt just as upset. He was getting to know Charlie by now; the little dog had a happy and outgoing nature. But a bad fright like this could spoil his temperament for a long time, maybe permanently.

Linda looked up as Bob went over to her.

"I can't tell you how sorry I am," said Bob, before she had a chance to speak.

"It's not good enough, Mr. Parker," said Linda. "Next time I go away, Charlie will go back to Pretty Paws."

She got up, ignored Bob when he tried to help her, called to Tansy, and stalked back to her car.

The only dog owner left was Mr. Smith. His Jack Russell had settled down and was sitting at his feet. Neil had expected him to walk off in a huff like all the others, but he just smiled. "Well, that was quite a scene," he said. "Why do you keep a cat, Mr. Parker, with all these dogs around."

"It's not our cat," said Bob.

For the first time Neil had the chance to ask himself where the cat had come from. He had never seen it before. And how had it gotten into the barn? He was sure it hadn't been there when he and Emily had cleaned up earlier.

Slowly, he walked back to the barn and stood in the doorway looking in. Everything was quiet now. Sunlight slanted in from the windows and shone on the bales of straw. Neil thought he heard a faint movement from behind the stack.

"Is someone there?" he called.

Silence. Neil almost went out again, but instead he moved cautiously down the length of the barn, listening hard and trying not to make any noise himself. There was a sudden scuffling, and then the unmistakable sound of a sneeze.

"Who's there?" Neil demanded.

He reached the stack and heaved one of the bales aside. Crouching in the space behind it were Amanda and Toby Sparrow.

"Okay," said Bob Parker. "Let me get this straight. You walked across the fields from your house with your own cat in a pet carrier, hid in the barn, and then let it out in the middle of my class with the deliberate intention of wrecking it?"

"S'pose so," Amanda muttered, shuffling her feet. Toby, his eyes and nose streaming from allergies, said nothing.

Neil had rarely seen his father so angry. He had marched the Sparrow children into the office and made them admit what they had done.

"I suppose it didn't occur to you that you were being cruel to your cat? The dogs scared him half to death. And suppose one of them had caught him? Did you ever think about that?"

Amanda shook her head. Toby started to sob.

"I'm going to phone your mom for her to come get you. As for the cat — Neil, go and see if Emily has managed to get him out of the tree."

Neil slipped out as Bob picked up the phone. In the yard, he was just in time to see the black cat scramble down the tree and push its face into the bowl of food that Emily had put at the bottom. Emily stroked him as he ate.

"Poor cat," she said. "What a rotten thing to do. Be careful, Neil, don't frighten him."

Neil stopped a few paces away. "Those two deliberately wrecked Dad's class. That's much worse than anything we did at Pretty Paws."

"I should never have given them that flyer," said Emily.

"Don't start blaming yourself," Neil said indignantly. "It's not your fault. They just don't care about animals at all!"

Emily sighed, still stroking the cat. "They got what they wanted, though. We've lost Charlie again. And all the other owners."

"No, one of them stayed. Mom's showing Mr. Smith around the kennels now."

"That's good."

It took some time to coax the frightened cat into the Sparrows' pet carrier. When Neil and Emily carried it back to the house, they found Bob waiting with the Sparrow children for their mother to arrive.

Toby poked a finger through the grill on the front of the carrier. "Hey, Sable," he whispered. "Are you OK?"

"You don't really care!" Emily said hotly.

Toby pulled his hand back and gave her a miserable look.

They didn't have long to wait before the pink minivan pulled into the driveway. Mrs. Sparrow got out. She was furious. She took the pet carrier from Emily and snapped at Toby and Amanda to get into the car.

"I'm very sorry about this, Mr. Parker," she said.

"I'm sorry, too." Bob's tone was calm, but Neil could tell that he was still very angry. "I've lost valuable business because of them. More important, Linda Woodham's Charlie and your own cat were both badly frightened — you're lucky it wasn't worse." His voice hardened. "Please make sure Toby and Amanda stay away from here in the future. In fact," he added, "I think the less Pretty Paws and King Street have to do with each other in the future, the better it will be for all of us."

CHAPTER EIGHT

Neil was in the office the next morning updating the Puppy Patrol web site on the computer when he heard a furious banging on the front door. "It never stops!" he muttered to himself. Sighing, he pushed back his chair and went to answer it.

When he opened the front door he could do nothing but stare. Standing on the step was Toby Sparrow — the last person he had expected to see!

"What are you doing here?" he asked when he had got over the first shock. "You'd better hope Dad doesn't catch you. He told you to stay away."

Toby's face was red, and sweat plastered his brown hair to his forehead. His bike lay abandoned in the driveway at the bottom of the front steps. He had unhooked the pet carrier, removed the top, and thrust it under Neil's nose. "Look!" he said.

In the basket were three tiny puppies. They were squirming and whimpering thin, feeble cries. Neil could see they were far too young to be away from their mother.

"Where did you get those?" he asked.

"We found them outside the gate when we went over to Pretty Paws this morning," Toby said. "Somebody must have left them there."

"And why did you bring them here?"

Toby's mouth trembled as if he was going to cry. "We've nowhere to keep them," he explained. "Mom said she'd take them to the police, but they won't be able to look after them properly. I'd do it myself, but I don't know how!" He pushed the basket into Neil's hands. "You've got to take them, or they'll die!"

Neil looked at Toby and then at the feebly wriggling puppies. "You'd better come in," he said.

Neil took Toby into the kitchen. The room was empty, except for Sam asleep in his basket. Neil put the puppies down on the kitchen table and went to look out of the back door. Carole and Emily were on their way across the yard with Jake and some of the boarding dogs on leashes.

"Hey, Mom!" said Neil. "Come and see what I've got."

Carole and Emily came into the kitchen after

they'd kenneled the dogs. Carole stopped short when she saw Toby, and Emily said, "You again? What do you want?"

"No, it's OK," Neil said. "Look what he brought us."

As soon as Carole set eyes on the puppies, she went into action. She put a pan on the stove and started to heat some milk and took a couple of baby feeding bottles from one of the cabinets. This wasn't the first time she had rescued abandoned puppies.

"Emily," she said, "get me a basket from the storeroom. Neil, go and call Mike Turner. Try his home number. Ask him to come here — these puppies aren't strong enough to be moved anymore."

Neil called and managed to catch the vet at home; he promised to come right away. When he went back into the kitchen Emily had appeared with the basket, and Toby was explaining to Carole how he came to have the puppies. He looked calmer now that the puppies were being cared for.

"Will they die?" he asked anxiously.

"I hope not," said Carole. "But they'll need a lot of care. They should never have been left out like that."

"Somebody who'd do that isn't fit to have a dog," said Neil.

Carole tested the heat of the milk with a few drops on her wrist and stirred a spoonful of sugar into it. "Do you want to help feed them?" she asked Toby.

Toby went pink again. "Can I?"

"You'll have to be very careful. Sit down and take one on your lap."

Toby did as she said and tried to insert the bottle into the puppy's mouth. The puppy whimpered and pulled his head away. "He won't take it!" Toby said, dismayed.

"Here, try this." Carole squeezed a few drops of milk onto her fingers and smeared it over the puppy's lips. The puppy licked at it, suddenly seemed to catch on, and began sucking eagerly. Toby's face broke into a smile.

"Not too much at first," Carole warned. "Here, Emily, you do another one."

"Squirt would go wild for this!" Neil said, grinning. "Where is she, anyway?"

"*Sarah* is watching your dad's obedience class in the barn." Carole glanced at Toby, who had suddenly started to look uncomfortable again. "Let's hope we don't have any extra livestock in there this time."

Toby shook his head. Carole lifted up the puppy, who was now looking sleepy and contented, and gave him the third one to feed. "Does your mother know you're here?" she asked.

"No. Nobody does."

"I'd better give her a call."

"She'll kill me," Toby said. "But I don't care. I had to do something!"

"Well, you did the right thing," said Carole. "I'll try to make her see that."

"What will happen to the puppies now?" Toby asked, gently stroking the head of the one he was feeding.

"We'll find them homes," said Neil.

While Carole went to find some old blankets for the puppies' bedding, he and Emily explained to Toby how Bob had inherited some money and was using it to finance the rescue center.

"We won't ever have to worry about dogs being destroyed," said Emily. "They'll be safe here until someone comes along who wants them."

Toby stroked the puppy's head again. It had stopped sucking and gone to sleep in his lap. "I wonder if . . ." he began.

Neil and Emily exchanged a grin. It wasn't too difficult to see how Toby's mind was working. Neil couldn't help wondering, though, if the Sparrows were fit to take care of a dog. Toby wasn't so bad, maybe, but there was still that awful Amanda!

"Mrs. Parker," Toby said, when Carole came back with the blankets, "what kind of dogs are these?"

"It's hard to tell when they're so tiny," said Carole. "They're probably mixed breeds."

She made a nest of blankets in the basket and put it down close to the stove. Toby and Emily carefully laid the puppies inside it. They wriggled into a heap and went to sleep.

"There," said Carole. "If they're kept warm and well fed, I think they'll be fine." She gave a wry smile. "Guess who'll have to get up in the middle of the night to feed them?"

"Do you really do that?" Toby was round-eyed.

Carole shrugged. "Somebody has to. Neil, why don't you take Toby and show him around? Mike Turner will want some peace and quiet to examine the puppies."

"Okay," said Neil.

He and Emily led Toby out into the yard.

"That's the barn," he said, waving a hand at it as they walked past. "That's where Dad gives his obedience classes — but you know that, don't you?"

"I'm really sorry," Toby said in a small voice.

"Don't nag him, Neil," said Emily. "He knows now it was stupid. Let's not say any more about it." She patted Toby's shoulder comfortingly. "Let's go and see the new rescue center."

Neil pulled open the door of the circular building and led Toby into a wedge-shaped space that narrowed to an opening in the middle. There were cabinets down one side, a sink, and a countertop.

"This is the storage and work area," he explained. "We can prepare the rescue dogs' food here and bathe them if they need it."

"No more running across from the kennel blocks in the pouring rain!" said Emily.

The center of the building was a circular space with the doors of the pens leading off it.

"Fifteen pens," said Neil, "so we can look after fifteen dogs at once. When they're in the pens they can see each other, so they don't get lonely, but they can't reach one another."

He opened the door of one of the pens and went inside. "There's underground heating, and that door at the end leads into the outside run."

"It's terrific!" said Toby, gazing around in admiration. "Far better than —" He broke off and looked embarrassed.

"Pretty Paws looks good, too," said Emily kindly.

"Well, the front's okay, but —"

Neil interrupted him to say, "It's not just how the place looks that matters, it's how you treat the dogs."

He led the way outside again and over toward the old rescue center. Eddie and Dan and the other builders were sitting outside, drinking coffee. There was no sign of Pooh-Bah. Dan had started leaving him in the spare pen in the rescue center. He hadn't said any more about finding him another home, and Neil hoped he still wanted to keep the Peke even after Pooh-Bah had been so disobedient at the class.

"When we open the new rescue center," Neil went on, trying to forget Pooh-Bah's problems, "the old center is going to be a dog clinic. Mike Turner is going to come one morning a week to begin with, to give advice about dog problems, and we're looking for a full-time staff member to work alongside Kate."

"The rescue center will be a registered charity, too," said Emily.

"You do so much," said Toby. "Dogs are your whole lives."

"That's the way we like it," Neil agreed.

"I wish *we* . . ." Toby stopped again and looked at his feet.

"You could do a lot more," Neil said. "Just you, if you wanted to. You could learn more about looking after dogs. No more chocolate, for a start. Maybe if you did that, your mom and Amanda would get the idea."

"I'll lend you some magazines to read," Emily offered.

Toby brightened up. "Well, I could try."

"Great!" Neil gave him a friendly punch on the shoulder. "Come on, I'll show you the rescue dogs."

When Toby had left, his bike basket crammed with Emily's dog magazines, Neil and Emily went back into the kitchen. The obedience class was over, and Sarah was cooing over the puppies.

"Can we keep them?" she asked Carole.

"Sarah, you know we can't. Wash your hands for lunch," she said. "And someone go and find your dad."

As she was speaking, Bob Parker came into the kitchen. Neil thought he had a funny look on his face.

"Do you know who I've been talking to?" Bob tugged his beard thoughtfully. "On the phone just now?"

"No, who?" Carole asked.

"Mrs. Fitz."

"What did she want?"

"She was really upset. I thought she was going to start crying. She seemed to think she had to apologize to me for sending Sheba to Pretty Paws." While he talked, he pulled a tray of garlic bread out of the oven and started transferring it to a serving dish. "She got back from her daughter's last night and picked Sheba up, and she said . . . You remember how nervous Sheba used to be of other dogs?"

"She's been much better lately," said Emily.

"Not anymore, according to Mrs. Fitz," Bob told her. "She was crying — Sheba, I mean — the whole night, and Mrs. Fitz had to sit up with her. Mrs. Fitz says the biggest mistake she ever made was sending Sheba to Pretty Paws. She's even talking about writing to the paper about them. She asked if we would forgive her and let Sheba come here again next time."

"So what did you say?" Neil asked, fascinated.

"Well, of course I said yes. And I invited her to our grand opening on Saturday. That seemed to cheer her up. But what I'd like to know," he added, as everyone sat around the table, "is what happened to Sheba at Pretty Paws to make her so upset?"

"Neil, I've been thinking," said Emily.

Lunch was over; she and Neil had sneaked out to the yard with Jake and Sam to avoid the washing-up.

"What about?"

"All this business with Mrs. Fitz and Sheba getting frightened at Pretty Paws. Did you notice what Toby said when we were talking about Pretty Paws? Something like, "The front's okay, but — and then you interrupted him because you were showing off."

"I wasn't!" Neil blushed.

"You were. Well, the front's okay but what? The

front's okay but around the back it's a mess? Around the back, we frighten dogs into fits?"

"We never went around the back," said Neil.

"We never got the chance," said Emily. "So I want to go and look."

Neil stared at her. She had a very obstinate look on her face, which made him slightly anxious. He knew from experience that when Emily made her mind up, it was very difficult to change it.

"Are you out of your mind?" he asked. "If we're caught around there again, Dad will take us into the barn and string us up by the ears!"

"There's something wrong there," Emily insisted. "Neil Parker, are you saying that you don't care?"

Neil thought. "You're right," he said. "We've got to do it."

CHAPTER NINE

Neil and Emily didn't have the chance to slip away
to visit Pretty Paws until after dinner on the following Tuesday. With any luck, they hoped the Sparrows would have gone home and only Pauline would
be around.

"No, Sam, not this time," Neil said, as the Border
collie got up, wagging his tail when he realized they
were going out. "We've got to be really quick and
quiet. Anyway, that Pauline might catch you and
give you a perm!"

While they were getting their bikes, Dan came
into the driveway on his way home, with Pooh-Bah
on a leash. The little Peke was darting here and
there, trying to sniff at all the fascinating smells

around him, but at least he was going more or less where Dan wanted him to go.

Dan was whistling cheerfully. "Hi, there," he said as he walked past.

"Hello," said Neil. "How's Pooh-Bah?" He didn't dare mention the obedience class.

"Great," Dan said contentedly. "Just great." He bent down to scratch the Peke's orange hair, and Pooh-Bah jumped up and pawed at his knees.

Neil stared at how friendly they were together.

"Then are you going to keep him?" Emily asked.

"Keep him? Of course I'm going to keep him. He's a great little dog!"

Neil and Emily exchanged a glance. Pride in his dog was just bursting out of Dan. Neil couldn't think what had happened to stop him being so embarrassed. "Er . . . yes," he said. "What did you . . ."

"Did you see the way he went for that cat the other day? He wasn't scared at all. This dog's got guts!" Dan bent down to ruffle Pooh-Bah's ears. Pooh-Bah panted up at him eagerly, pink tongue hanging out. "You know," said Dan, "I think I might change his name. Fang would be a good name, don't you think? It sounds really fierce."

Neil saw Emily slowly turning pink in her efforts not to laugh. Straight-faced, he said, "I don't think you can do that, Dan. Pooh-Bah knows his name. He wouldn't understand if you changed it."

Disappointment briefly crossed Dan's face, and

then he grinned. "It doesn't matter. It's what's inside that matters. Isn't that right?" he asked Pooh-Bah. "Just let Horace try laughing at you now!"

"You aren't going to let him chase cats, are you, Dan?" Emily asked, looking a bit worried.

"No, I won't let him hurt them. I'm going to book him for one of your dad's courses."

"Good," said Neil. He bent down and offered Pooh-Bah a dog treat. The Peke ate it up out of his palm. "He's bright enough. I'm sure he'll do well."

"Of course he will," said Dan. "See you."

He strode off, with the little Peke waddling along beside him.

"There goes Fang," said Neil, "dreaded cat-slayer of Compton." He grinned. "Well, at least we don't have to worry about them anymore."

This time the wrought-iron gate into Pretty Paws was locked.

"Bend down," said Emily. "We'll have to climb the wall."

Sighing, Neil bent over and grasped his ankles so that Emily could climb on his back; she straddled the top of the wall and reached a hand down to pull him up. They dropped lightly into the courtyard.

Everything was quiet. Neil couldn't see any movement from the windows of the apartment. Maybe even Pauline had gone out. It wouldn't have surprised him. Swiftly, Neil sprinted across the courtyard to the arched walkway leading through the stable block, with Emily at his heels. Once in the shelter of the tunnel, he felt he could relax.

"So far, so good," he muttered. "Now let's see what they're hiding around the back."

Cautiously, he crept down the path and looked out at the other end. Here there was a second courtyard leading to the stretch of rough ground. On either side was another pair of kennel blocks like the ones at the front.

From here, the look of Pretty Paws was very different. Grass was growing between the cobblestones. There were no flowers or fresh white paint. The woodwork was bare and rotten in places, as if it needed repair. Overflowing trash bins stood against one wall.

"It's a dump! said Emily.

Neil walked over to the left-hand kennel block and opened the door. It was empty and obviously disused; the floor was thick with dust.

"Well, if they're not putting dogs here . . ." Emily said, obviously relieved.

Loud barking cut off what she was saying. Neil spun around. The noise was coming from the right-hand kennel block. He ran across the courtyard and went in.

As soon as the outer door opened, an enormous German shepherd in the first pen launched itself at Neil and thumped against the pen door. Neil took a

step back, jostling Emily. For a second he had been afraid that the door would not hold.

The German shepherd was barking furiously. It was rearing up on its hind legs, its front paws splayed out against the wire. There was a savage look in its eyes. Neil was hardly ever afraid of a dog, but he was very glad there was a wire fence between him and this one.

Suddenly, Emily, who was peering over Neil's shoulder, exclaimed, "Oh, no!" and darted past Neil to the next pen down the row. "Neil, look! It's Charlie!"

Neil stared. The little golden retriever was crouched

close to the ground, cowering against the wire on the opposite side of the pen from the German shepherd.

"He's terrified," said Emily. She grasped the pen door and rattled it. "We've got to get him out of here!"

But the door was locked. Neil tried wrenching it away from its fastenings, hoping it was old enough to give way, but it held. The German shepherd still went on barking. Now that he was closer Neil could see that the water bowl in the pen was dry, as if no one had given the dog water for some time. That could be one of the reasons why it was so savage.

Emily was kneeling on the ground, trying to reach out to Charlie through the mesh. The puppy crawled along the wire toward her until she could just manage to touch his head. She was crying. "Neil, what have they done to him? We can't leave him here."

"Calm down, Em," said Neil. He was furious, but he had to keep his cool. "We'll get him out of here and take him home."

"But we can't get the door open."

"You stay here with him," Neil said. "I'll go and look for the key or wire-cutters. If I don't find anything, I'll get to a phone and call Dad."

He walked back down to the main courtyard. The office would be the first place to look, he thought, if he could get in. But before he could even try, he heard voices ahead of him in the courtyard.

"I don't know," the first voice said. Neil recognized

Pauline. "The dogs are always barking. It doesn't mean anything."

Huh! Neil thought, and then froze as he heard the second voice. "Maybe we should have a look."

Neil peered out the archway to make sure he was right in what he suspected. His eyes widened. The owner of the second voice, just as he had thought, was Jake Fielding, a young photographer from the *Compton News.*

Before Neil could draw back into the shelter of the walkway, Pauline spotted him.

"Hey!" she called. "You there! Come out!"

Neil took a few steps out into the courtyard, toward Pauline and Jake.

"Neil Parker!" Pauline exclaimed. "You were told to stay away from here. Just you wait till Mrs. Sparrow finds out about this."

Neil's mind was working furiously. "Hi, Pauline," he said. "Hi, Jake."

"You know Jake?" Pauline said sharply.

"Oh, yes," said Neil. "Jake and I are old friends. You do know who he is, don't you?"

Pauline went pink and simpered. "Of course I do!"

Neil grinned at Jake. The young photographer was scarlet from neck to hairline. Neil said, "He works for the *Compton News.*"

Pauline's mouth dropped open. She turned to Jake. "You told me —"

"I asked you for coffee," said Jake. "Strictly business. I'm sorry if you got the wrong idea."

"You . . ." Pauline was at a loss for words. She took a breath and finally managed to ask, "What is it you want, then?"

"I thought I'd take a look around," Jake explained. "Someone wrote to the *Compton News,* complaining about the noise and suggesting the dogs here are ill-treated."

CHAPTER TEN

As Jake finished speaking, the wrought-iron gate swung open and Mrs. Sparrow came in, followed by Toby and Amanda. Seeing the group by the archway, she strode straight across to them. "What's going on? Neil, what are you doing here?"

Neil thought that she didn't sound as angry as he would have expected. Even Amanda didn't have the horrible sneer on her face, and Toby was smiling happily.

"Hi, Neil," he said. "We've been reading your magazines. Me and Amanda, we both want to start helping properly. Mom brought us over to see what we could do."

"Great," Neil said, delighted.

"We're all really grateful that your mom and dad

could help with those puppies," Mrs. Sparrow said. "I
didn't want them to die, but I didn't know what to do
for them." She hesitated and then asked, "Maybe we
could all make a new start."

If she had said that before he found Charlie and
the German shepherd in the back kennel block, Neil
would have agreed wholeheartedly. Now he was not
so sure. "I think you'd better talk to Dad," he said.

"Yes, I —" Mrs. Sparrow began to say and broke off
as she spotted Jake Fielding. "Hello — can I help you?"

Jake glanced at Pauline, but she was just looking
sulky. He held out a hand to Mrs. Sparrow. "Hi. I'm
Jake Fielding."

"From the *Compton News*," Neil added.

As if on cue, another spate of furious barking came
from the German shepherd in the back courtyard.
Mrs. Sparrow gave a sharp glance down the walkway. She sounded anxious as she said, "And what can
I do for you, Mr. Fielding?"

"Someone wrote to the paper complaining about
the way you treat your dogs," Jake said. "Do you
have any comments about that, Mrs. Sparrow?"

Mrs. Sparrow drew herself up. "Anyone who wants
to complain can complain to me, not the press. You
won't find any dogs ill-treated at Pretty Paws." She
pointed to one of the kennel blocks. "Take a look, if
you like."

Neil almost said, "Try the one around the back."
Bad publicity was no more than Mrs. Sparrow de-

served for what she had done to Charlie. While he hesitated, Jake said, "That won't be necessary. I can see everything *here* is fine."

The way he said *here* made Neil pretty sure he knew that something was wrong somewhere. Neil said, "Jake —"

Mrs. Sparrow started to speak and broke off. Toby and Amanda exchanged worried looks. Neil suddenly found that he couldn't give them away. Not at the moment when Toby and Amanda had just decided to make a real effort with the dogs.

"Neil?" Jake was waiting. "Did you want to tell me something?"

"Tell you . . . er . . . no." Neil was floundering, trying to think what to say. "Just — just to ask if you're coming to our grand opening on Saturday."

Jake looked disappointed, although he tried to hide it with a smile. "Sure, Neil. I wouldn't miss it for the world."

"So if that's all, Mr. Fielding," Mrs. Sparrow said, "I've got things to do. . . . "

"Of course." Jake raised a hand in farewell. "Thanks for your time. See you, Pauline."

Pauline tossed her head and said nothing as the young photographer strolled across the courtyard and vanished through the gate.

"Pauline," Mrs. Sparrow said when he had gone, "bringing the press in here wasn't a very smart thing to do, was it?"

"I didn't know he was the press," Pauline defended herself.

"You obviously didn't know who he was. Pauline, it's very important that we don't —"

"Never mind Jake," Neil interrupted. He wasn't prepared to wait while Mrs. Sparrow and Pauline had an argument. "What are you going to do about that?" He jerked his head toward the back courtyard, where the German shepherd was still barking loudly.

"Oh, I know," Mrs. Sparrow said, distressed. "It's not an ideal place to put him. But he made so much noise, and he really frightened Mrs. Fitz's Sheba when she was here. I thought it wouldn't do any harm to kennel him away from the other dogs."

Neil stared at her and suddenly realized that Mrs. Sparrow had no idea what was going on in her own kennels. Toby and Amanda looked just as puzzled.

"I think you'd better come and look," he said.

They all followed him down the path and into the other kennel block, where Emily was still crouched beside the wire trying to comfort Charlie. The German shepherd sprang up against the wire again as the door opened.

Emily looked up, her face still streaked with tears. "Get him out!" she said to Mrs. Sparrow. "He's terrified. You're cruel to put him in here."

"But I didn't . . ." Mrs. Sparrow had gone white. She pulled a bunch of keys out of her handbag and unlocked the pen. Emily pushed her way in, sat be-

side Charlie, and held him close. Toby squatted beside her and stroked Charlie's head.

Mrs. Sparrow turned to Pauline. "Why is Charlie in here?" she asked coldly.

"I just put him in here for a little while," Pauline explained. "While I cleaned out his pen. I didn't think it would do any harm."

"But you weren't cleaning out his pen," Neil pointed out. "You were chatting with Jake Fielding. And why doesn't the German shepherd have any water?"

Pauline stared. "You don't think I'm going in there

with that brute, do you? I don't want to get bitten, thanks very much!"

Neil almost laughed. Pauline had at last met something she couldn't call a "sweet little doggy," and she didn't like it one bit.

"Pauline," Mrs. Sparrow said, sounding tired, "it's probably my fault, but I don't really think you can cope with this job, can you? I think you'd better leave at the end of the month."

"Don't worry, I will!" said Pauline.

She flounced out of the kennel block. When the click of her heels had died away down the path, Mrs. Sparrow sighed and said, "Neil, Emily, I'm really sorry. I had no idea. . . . And now what are we going to do about Captain here?"

"His owner will kill us if he finds him like this!" said Amanda.

Neil eyed the German shepherd. He was quiet now and was standing in the pen with head down and jaws gaping as he panted. He knew it was vital to give the dog water, but he also knew there would be a risk to anyone who opened the pen. Captain might have been no more than noisy to begin with, but neglect had turned him savage.

"Mrs. Sparrow," he said, "I think you'd better give my dad a call."

"I blame myself," said Mrs. Sparrow.

The Sparrows and the Parkers were sitting around

the kitchen table at King Street Kennels. It was the day after Neil and Emily's discoveries at Pretty Paws.

Sarah grabbed Toby and dragged him over to the basket where the puppies he had rescued were wriggling contentedly. She and Toby played with them while the others talked. Bob Parker handed around cups of coffee and glasses of orange juice.

When Mrs. Sparrow had telephoned him, Bob had driven to Pretty Paws right away. He had managed to get into Captain's pen to give the German shepherd food and water, and the dog had settled down. Neil thought he must have been exhausted.

Meanwhile, Toby and Amanda, under Neil's supervision, had cleaned out the pen Charlie should have been using. Neil had felt a lot of satisfaction in seeing Amanda with her hands dirty; to be fair, she hadn't made a fuss.

Emily had taken Charlie to run and play on the rough ground at the back of Pretty Paws, and, when the little retriever was finally put in his pen, he had recovered a lot of his natural cheerfulness. All the same, Neil wouldn't be happy until he was sure that there was no permanent damage to Charlie's gentle temperament.

Mrs. Sparrow took a sip of coffee and sighed. "I should have known Pauline wasn't fit to be left in charge," she admitted. "But she was good with the little dogs, and she did make them look pretty." She looked embarrassed and added, "I know you think it's silly."

"I think you're going over the top," Carole said frankly. "These are dogs, not toys. I know some owners are stupid, but that doesn't mean we have to encourage them." More kindly, she added, "You could still offer a really good professional grooming service. It's more than we have time for here."

Mrs. Sparrow shook her head worriedly. "I don't know if I can carry on."

"Oh, come on," Bob said encouragingly. "It's not as bad as all that."

"I let both those dogs down. Charlie and Captain."

When she said that, Neil suddenly warmed to Mrs. Sparrow. At least she understood what she'd done and wasn't trying to make excuses for herself. "Nobody needs to know about it," he said. "We won't tell. And Jake Fielding didn't see."

"I'm very grateful to you, Neil," Mrs. Sparrow said, with a faint smile. "But I must still tell the two owners what happened — Captain's and Linda Woodham."

"That would be best," Bob agreed. "And maybe you shouldn't use the pens in the back courtyard in the future."

"I didn't mean to," Mrs. Sparrow explained, "until we could afford to expand and have it cleaned up properly. But when Captain made so much noise and was upsetting other dogs, it seemed the only way of getting him away from them. He would have been fine if he'd been properly fed."

"I think he would," Bob said and added gently, "but it was your responsibility to see to it."

"I know." For a minute Mrs. Sparrow looked as if she might cry. Amanda leaned over and gave her mom's hand a squeeze.

"Look," said Bob, "I don't see any reason why you can't make a fresh start. You need properly qualified help. Maybe someone who has taken the Kennel Staff Certificate course. Kate McGuire, who works for me, says it's really good."

"Well, if I could find someone . . ."

"I'll give you a hand," Bob promised. "And you could improve your own skills. Have you ever thought of getting the Diploma of Kennel Management?"

Mrs. Sparrow shook her head. She looked bewildered. Neil would have bet that she'd never even heard of the Diploma of Kennel Management. "I just love dogs," she said.

"Well, that's a start," said Carole. "But it's not enough by itself."

"I know that now." Mrs. Sparrow looked ashamed.

"Don't worry," said Bob. "We'll all help, won't we?"

"Sure we will," said Emily.

"We'll train a couple of extra kennel assistants," Neil said. "Toby and Amanda!"

Amanda made a face at him, but it was a friendly face. *Maybe she wasn't so bad when you got to know her,* Neil thought. But he still didn't particularly *want* to get to know her.

"Well, if I do carry on," said Mrs. Sparrow, "I think I'll concentrate on smaller breeds. Captain was a bit much for me to handle."

"Good idea," Bob said. "And maybe we could work together, not as rivals. We could recommend owners to send their dogs to the place that's most suitable for them." He grinned. "You can have Sugar and Spice, for a start."

"Oh, those awful little Westies!" Mrs. Sparrow exclaimed. "Do you know, they tore their cushions apart! You should have seen the pen!"

"Typical Sugar and Spice!" said Emily.

Toby looked up from the floor where he was playing with the puppies he had rescued. Two of them were crawling over him, and he had a blissful smile on his face. "Mom," he said, "can I have one of these puppies when they're ready? Please?"

Mrs. Sparrow smiled and began, "Well . . ."

"I wouldn't recommend it," said Bob. "I had a chat about these little fellows with Mike Turner. He thinks they're going to grow up into *big* fellows, and they probably have some rottweiler in them. They'll be dogs for experienced owners, not for children."

Toby looked upset. He stroked the nearest puppy sadly.

Mrs. Sparrow looked almost as upset as Toby. "We always said we would have a dog when we moved out to the country," she said. "That's one reason we didn't want to live in the apartment at Pretty Paws."

"Well, that's no problem," said Bob. "I'm always hearing about dogs that need a good home. Cheer up, Toby. If your mom agrees, I'm sure the right dog for you will come along really soon."

Music came from the Parkers' exercise field, where Paul Hamley, the principal of Meadowbank School, had set up the school's public address system. As Neil listened, the music was replaced by a voice announcing the results of one of the pet show classes.

With Jake trotting beside him, Neil hurried up to the side gate, which had been replaced along with the section of fencing. Above the gate was a banner reading *King Street Kennels Rescue Center: Grand*

Opening! Carole Parker was standing underneath it with Sam at her feet, greeting people as they came in. As Neil approached, she shook hands with Jane Hammond. Jane owned Delilah, the black and white Border collie who was Jake's mom. Sam and Delilah nuzzled each other affectionately.

"Hi, Jane," said Neil. "Jake, say hello to your mom." As Jake and Delilah touched noses, he told Carole, "Dad says to get everyone around the rescue center. The ceremony's due to start in about ten minutes."

"Okay. Is Max ready?"

Neil pointed to the path that led up to the new rescue center. Max Hooper, the star of *The Time Travelers,* was signing autographs for his excited fans. Prince, his golden cocker spaniel, was darting from one to another, reveling in all the attention he was getting.

"Just as soon as his fans let him go," Neil said.

People were already starting to drift over from the exercise field and more were still pouring through the gates. Neil said hello to Dr. Harvey and his two dogs, Finn and Sandy. Just behind them, Neil was delighted to see Linda Woodham, with Tansy and Charlie on their leashes.

Linda came up with an enormous smile. "She did it!" she announced. "Tansy did it! She was Best in Show at the big Salford dog event, so now she's a Show Champion."

Neil bent down to rumple the ears of the adult dog and offered her a dog treat. "Well done, girl!" He laughed as Charlie came pushing in, planted one paw against Neil's knee, and demanded his share.

"Is he okay?" Neil asked, giving him a tidbit. There was no trace of nervousness in the puppy's happy, alert look.

"Yes, fine," Linda said. "Mrs. Sparrow told me everything when I picked him up. I'm very grateful to you, Neil. And Carole — Tansy has one more show, next week, and Mrs. Sparrow herself said I ought to bring Charlie here to King Street. Will that be all right?"

"Yes, of course," said Carole. "See me when all this is over, and I'll make a definite booking for you."

Linda smiled down at Charlie, who was still doing his best to climb up Neil's leg. "I think Charlie made his choice a long time ago!" she said.

Still smiling, she went with Charlie and Tansy into the crowd. Carole began directing people over to the new rescue center for the opening ceremony. Neil spotted Kate McGuire and her boyfriend, Glen; Eddie Thomas and his wife, Maureen, with their dog, Blackie; and Dan with Pooh-Bah.

It seemed as if all their friends, dogs, and owners had come to King Street to celebrate with them.

Max gave back the last of the autograph books and came to join Neil. Neil scanned the crowds for his dad and saw Bob on his way in from the field. Emily

was with him and ran ahead when she saw Neil. She was laughing.

"Guess what? Mrs. Fitz and Sheba won the Pet Most Like Its Owner!"

"Oh . . ." said Neil. "Was Mrs. Fitz annoyed?"

"No, she was really pleased. She thinks Sheba's beautiful. Anyway," she continued, "she's much happier now. She says Sheba's getting over her nervousness again."

Bob came up, took out a pair of silver scissors in a leather case, and handed them to Max. "Ready to go?" he asked.

"Ready when you are," Max replied.

Jake Fielding, his camera slung around his neck, appeared out of the crowd. He seemed to have forgiven Neil for holding out on him at Pretty Paws. At any rate, he gave Neil a cheerful grin as he fished in his pocket for a spare lens.

"Okay," said Bob. "No — wait — where is everybody? Neil, where's your mom?"

"She was rounding everybody up."

He turned and saw Carole coming up the path, bringing Sarah, Sam, and Jake. With her were Mrs. Sparrow, Toby, and Amanda. Carole found them places to stand to watch the ceremony.

Still more friends were crowding around. Mike Turner, Terri McCall, Sergeant Moorhead from the local police, Pastor Gavin Thorpe with Jet, Chris Wilson and his parents, Julie Baker with her Old English sheepdog, Ben, Hasheem, and more of their classmates from Meadowbank School. Neil thought half of Compton must be there in a semicircle in front of the doors of the new rescue center.

A broad red ribbon was stretched across the doors, tied in a bow in the middle. Max stepped up to it, scissors at the ready.

Somebody in the crowd yelled, "Speech!" and Paul Hamley hurried up with a microphone for Max. Max took it and looked around; the crowd grew quieter.

"Hello, everyone," said Max. "I'm really honored to be here today to open this new rescue center for the

Parkers. You all know how much they've done for dogs in Compton, and now they'll be able to do even more."

He raised the scissors and slashed through the ribbon. The ends fluttered to the ground as Jake Fielding clicked his camera.

Max beamed as he announced, "I now declare the new King Street Kennels Rescue Center open!"

Hasheem shouted, "Three cheers for the Puppy Patrol!"

As he joined in the cheering, Neil felt that he wouldn't want to change places with anybody else in the whole world.